鷸蚌相爭 拒學記

文／孟瑛如
圖／梁雯媛
英文翻譯／吳侑達

蚌蚌阿肥看見美麗的陽光，就不自覺的張大了蚌殼，露出渾圓雪白的肚皮，想好好曬個太陽！正要去上學的鷸鳥花花經過時就想啄他，結果蚌蚌阿肥立刻「噗」一聲閉上了蚌殼，將鷸鳥花花長長的嘴給牢牢夾住了！

鷸鳥花花用力的將長嘴拔呀拔的，但還是拔不出來。於是，她便對蚌蚌阿肥說：「你快些鬆開蚌殼吧！如果一直待在這兒，要是今天不下雨，明天也不下雨，你就會乾死的！」

蚌蚌阿肥也對鷸鳥花花說：

「不！我不放開你。你啄不到我，也吃不到其他東西，你會先餓死的！而且你也不能上學了！」

鷸鳥花花一聽到蚌蚌阿肥說互咬著就可以不用上學，心裡竟然樂了起來，也不再掙扎著想將長嘴從蚌蚌阿肥的蚌殼裡拔出來了！反而好奇的問起蚌蚌阿肥為何不想上學？

蚌蚌阿肥立刻由緊閉的嘴裡模糊的吐出一連串不想上學的理由！

不想上學，因為校門口的小黃會一直瞪著我！
不想上學，因為要早起！
不想上學，因為老師總要我做很多事！
不想上學，因為有好多作業！
不想上學，因為不好玩！

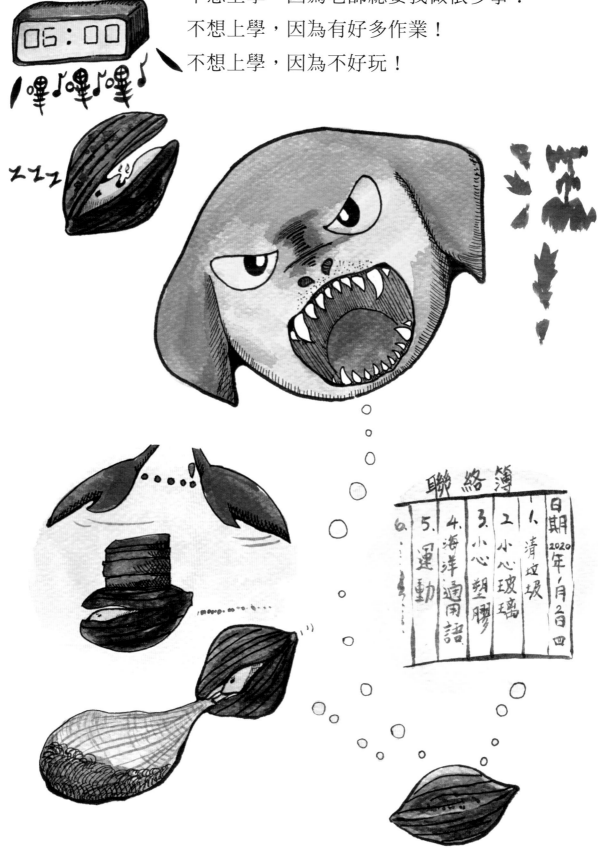

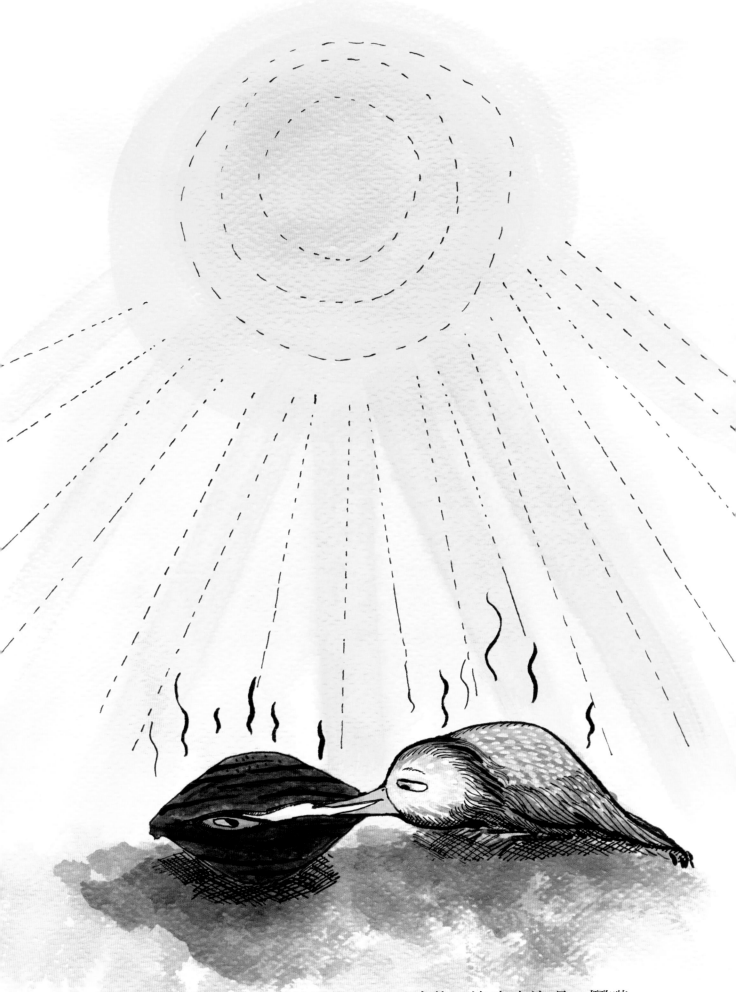

蚌蚌阿肥和鷸鳥花花就這樣整天互咬著，沒吃也沒喝，鬥嘴也鬥到沒力氣了！

直到太陽下山,學校也放學了,同學們陸陸續續經過姿勢看
起來很怪異、又疲累不堪的蚌蚌阿肥和鷸鳥花花!

當知道他們倆從早上開始就上演「鷸蚌相爭」的劇碼因而不能上學後，同學們決定輪流說一件上學的趣事，告訴他們一定要上學的一百種理由……

去上學，因為校門口的小黃會一直搖著尾巴歡迎我！

去上學，今天小黃還幫我咬著水壺進教室呢！

去上學，早起不遲到，從從容容吃完早餐，還可以跟路上的
鳥兒打招呼！

　　去上學，早起動動精神好☺，
還可以跟一大群同學同時**擠**進校門，
酷！

去上學，老師要我幫忙很多事，
我沒去上學，老師要怎麼辦呢？

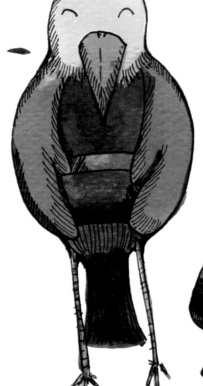

去上學，同學要我幫忙很多事，
我今天得了十五次謝謝呢！

去上學，我很喜歡幫忙大家呢！

去上學，昨天的作業很有趣，寫過的人才知道！

去上學，要寫作業才有話題跟同學討論！

去上學，爸媽每天接我回家的第一句話都是：「作業寫完沒？」如果沒有作業，爸媽就沒得問了！會很**可憐**！

去上學，我們班昨天上課表現好，又守規矩，得到秩序總冠軍呢！老師說要**大大**的獎勵我們！

去上學，昨天我們分組做實驗，好好玩、好刺激！

去上學，我們昨天打球狂勝隔壁班，好過癮！

去上學，下禮拜我們班要
一起煮火鍋吃，好期待！

去上學，我們還可以帶玩具來分享！

去上學，我說話才有好多人聽！

去上學，才有人看到我完成很難、卻沒有放棄的事！

去上學，……

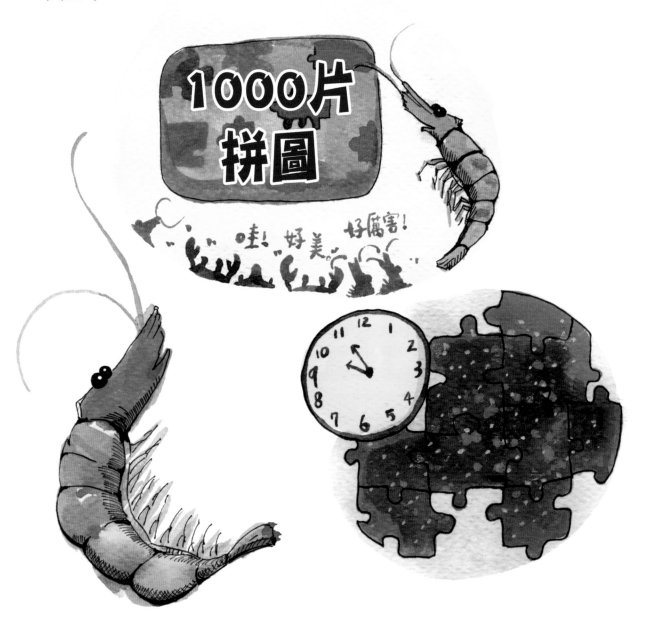

去上學，才可以找到很多人一起玩，可以看到很多花跟樹，可以看到自己種的菜，最重要的是能夠認識好朋友，還可以學會許多事！

　　每個人上學的理由有好多好多，但最重要的是，不去上學就沒機會做這些事了！

蚌蚌阿肥和鷸鳥花花聽到經過的同學你一言、我一語的說著上學趣事，又熱又渴的他們，想到自己除了被太陽曬還是被太陽曬的一天，加上互咬的愚蠢模樣，好像不只同學，連旁邊的花花草草都在嘲笑他們呢！

「爸媽上班有話說，我們上學有話說，只有
你們咬在一起沒話說，哈哈哈！」

蚌蚌阿肥和鷸鳥花花也開始想上學了，很想加入同學，
卻不知該如何找臺階下？也不知道該如何放開自己的嘴？

同學們圍成一圈鼓勵他們：「誰先鬆開嘴，誰就可以獲得上學的權利！」但蚌蚌阿肥和鷸鳥花花還是不知誰該先退讓！

同學們商量了一下，想到一個好主意，
大家一起大聲喊：
「一、二、三，鬆開！」
「一、二、三，鬆開！」
「一、二、三，鬆開！」
　終於，「**噗**」一聲……

蚌蚌阿肥鬆動痠麻的蚌殼，鷸鳥花花扶正差點歪掉的長嘴！他們終於放開彼此，也終於可以好好上學了！

　　我常常在親職演講的場合詢問爸媽：「為何要送孩子上學？」「上學的目的何在？」大多數爸媽會一下子愣住，彷彿我問了一個天經地義、但他們卻從未思考過，只是在人生歷程中照做的事情。若再詢問到：「覺得孩子喜歡上學嗎？」「最喜歡去上學做什麼事？」這類問題，大多數爸媽都是沉默以對，或是以懷疑的眼光看著我：「大家都要上學，需要問到這麼細嗎？」若是在拒學症、學校適應困難、分離焦慮或是社交恐懼症的個案場合，則會看到更多困惑、困擾、困頓、無所適從的爸媽，不能明白為何別人家的孩子去上學一點問題都沒有，但我家的孩子就是沒辦法好好上學呢？

　　教育哲學中對於教育的目的有許多看法，例如：學習社會的運作規則以融入社會、學習過群體生活、成為一個幸福的全人等。但臺灣的相關調查顯示，只有15%至21%的學童覺得「上學非常快樂」，大部分孩子根本不曉得為什麼要上學，就只是每天背著書包，跟著前去學校，然後再跟著回去家裡。而更多的爸媽及教師則經常是老生常談的告誡：「可以念書的時候不好好念，想當年我……」「不喜歡上學也要去，你以後要做個沒有用的人嗎？」「不能念書了，你才會珍惜……」如果我們的孩子只有在失去念書的機會或者離開學校以後，才能體會上學的快樂，那為何不先讓他們明瞭自己上學的目的並享受上學的樂趣，進而樂於上學與學習呢？

　　上學的快樂通常來自於學習、成長與人際互動三者，如果還沒發現其中的樂趣，可以及早尋找。做功課、準備考試很辛苦，但累積知識、學會技能的成就感與快樂，值得埋頭努力；學校管教、師長叮嚀很煩人，但認識自己、融入社會、開發潛能的快樂，擁有尊嚴與自主的生活，值得虛心受教。而上學的快樂大多數是來自社會性的快樂，也就是在人際互動和團體生活中所產生的快樂。一般而言，一個不喜歡上學的孩子，幾乎都是在學校得不到重視、肯定、鼓勵，甚至被忽略、貶抑或排斥的孩子。

　　所以說，要讓孩子喜歡上學，最重要的方法之一，就是讓他們在學校得到重視、肯定與鼓勵，包括來自同學與師長的回饋。尤其是正向且具體的回饋，收效更大，會讓孩子更清楚知道未來該如何遵循社會所重視的價值，以充分發展自己的潛能，更能由學習過程中享受樂趣、尋求協助，在遇到挫折時的復原力也會更強。因此，要讚美孩子的努力、策略和選擇，而非他們的天賦，不要再只是說：「你很棒！」「你很聰明！」等話語，而能在肯定其艱辛付出時說「你很努力啊！」肯定其耐心和堅持時說：「儘管很難，但最棒的是你沒放棄！」肯定其面對工作時積極向上的精神時說：「你做事的態度非常好！」表揚其合作精神時說：「你和同學合作得真好！」稱讚其領導力時說：「這件事情你很負責，而且做得很好！」肯定其開放虛心態度時說：「你能重視別人的意見，這點做得非常好！」

　　這個繪本是出自「鷸蚌相爭」的寓言故事，是在約二千三百年前的戰國時代，一個叫蘇代的人為了阻止趙國的趙惠王攻打燕國而對趙惠王說的話（當時有七個國家：齊、楚、燕、韓、趙、魏、秦），意思是如果趙國和燕國像鷸和蚌一樣互相鬥爭，最後只會讓強大的秦國像漁人般從中得益。這是許多人所共同知道的版本，而我將它轉化成「鷸蚌相爭」就不能去上學，鷸跟蚌都不能從中獲得利益，然後透過陸續經過同學的你一言、我一語，讓他們知道上學的目的與樂趣。不管孩子能從中間接收到的訊息為何，只要能找到上學的目的或是樂趣，孩子就比較能快樂上學去。所以在繪本故事尾聲有一句呈現了：「去上學，……」是刻意留下的空白句，可以在導讀的時候讓孩子自己接續完成語句，也是爸媽及教師可以補充的正向完成語句。也希望還未到就學年齡的孩子，能由此繪本發掘自己未來上學的目的和樂趣；而已在就學的孩子，更能由此繪本尋找自己心目中的上學目的和樂趣！

祝大家上學愉快！學習快樂！

We Don't Want to Go To School

Written by Ying-Ru Meng

Illustrated by Wen-Yuan Liang

Translated by Arik Wu

One sunny, bright day, a clam, named Fatty, was sitting out for a sunbath, with his snow-white, round "belly" out in broad daylight. A snipe, named Flowery, happened to pass by on her way to school and decided to peck at it, but Fatty instantly slammed his shells shut, gripping Flowery's beak in between with a loud "pop"!

Flowery did everything she could to pull out her beak, but in vain. "Let go of my beak! If it doesn't rain today, and it doesn't rain tomorrow, you will be a dead clam in no time," she said to Fatty.

"No! I'll never let go! If I don't let go, you won't be able to peck at me and can't eat anything. You will starve to death first and you can't go to school either!" Fatty responded.

It delighted Flowery to think that both of them would not need to go to school if they held on to each other like this, so she stopped pulling her beak out. Instead, she asked why Fatty did not want to go to school.

Fatty instantly murmured a list of reasons through his tightly shut shells···

"I don't want to go to school because the yellow-furred dog at the front gate always glares at me!"

"I don't want to go to school because I have to wake up early!"

"I don't want to go to school because Teacher always wants me to do a lot of things!"

"I don't want to go to school because there are way too many assignments!"

"I don't want to go to school because it's not fun at all!"

So Fatty and Flowery ended up holding on to each other the whole day, not eating or drinking anything and arguing till both of them were completely worn out.

When the sun went down, Fatty's and Flowery's classmates were also dismissed from school. Many of them walked past Flowery and Fatty, who still remained in that awkward position and were completely worn out.

Once their classmates knew what had been going on since the morning and why they could not make it to school, each of them offered to tell one reason why it would be fun to go to school …

"I love going to school! The yellow-furred dog at the front gate always greets me by wagging its tail!"

"I love going to school! That doggie actually brought my water bottle to the classroom today!"

"I love going to school! You get to wake up early, finish breakfast nice and early, and say hello to all the birds on your way to school!"

"I love going to school! It feels great to wake up early and limber up a little and you get to SQUEEZE your way through the front gate with heaps of other students!"

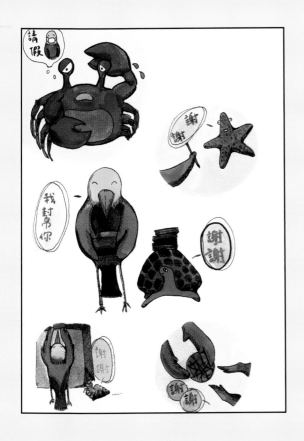

"I love going to school! Teacher always needs me to run errands for her. What does she do if I don't show up?"

"I love going to school! My classmates are always in great need of my help. I actually got thanked fifteen times today!"

"I love going to school! I love reaching out to help other people!"

"I love going to school! The assignment yesterday was a lot of fun! You wouldn't know if you didn't do it!"

"I love going to school! You will run out of things to talk about with your classmates if you don't get to do homework!"

"I love going to school because I'm afraid my parents will also run out of things to say. Every time when they pick me up from school, they always ask if I have finished my homework. They're going to be SAD if there's nothing to be worried about!"

"I love going to school! Our class just won an award yesterday for being the most disciplined and well-behaved and Teacher is going to reward us GREATLY!"

"I love going to school! We were doing a group science project yesterday and it was a lot of fun and excitement!"

"I love going to school! We straight up won a ball game against another class yesterday! By large margin! So fun!"

"I love going to school! Our class is going to throw a hot pot party next week! I can't wait!"

"I love going to school! We are even allowed to bring toys there to share with one another!"

"I love going to school because I'll have heaps of people hear what I have to say!"

"I love going to school because I'll have people witness how I persevere to overcome challenges!"

"I love going to school because⋯ "

Going to school allows us to hang out with many schoolmates, see many flowers and trees, look at vegetables planted by ourselves, and, most important of all, make heaps of friends and learn heaps of valuable knowledge! There are many, many reasons why we should go to school, but the most crucial of all is perhaps this: we will not be able to experience any of these if we do not go to school!

Hot and dehydrated, Fatty and Flowery suddenly realized that, while both of them were busy not letting go of each other and getting torched by the sun like two fools for the entire day, their classmates were actually having a lot of fun in school. It seemed like even the flowers and the grass were teasing them.

"Moms and dads go to work so they have things to talk about, and we go to school so we also have things to talk about. But the two of you are stuck here, having nothing new to talk about. Haha!"

Now that Fatty and Flowery realized what a mistake they had made, they were also dying to go back to school, to join their fellow classmates in having lots of fun. But they had no idea how to let go of each other and get out of this standoff without appearing even more foolish.

Their classmates surrounded the two of them and encouraged them to let go of each other. "Hey! Whoever lets go first gets to go back to school! Come on!" they said. Still, Fatty and Flowery did not know who should let go first.

Their classmates then came up with a brilliant idea. "One, two, three - let go!" every one of them started chanting. "One, two, three - let go!" "One, two, three - let go?"

Finally, with a loud "POP" ......

Fatty the Clam loosened up his already sore shells, and Flowery the Snipe also got to fix her almost skewed beak. The two of them could eventually go to school!